# EDGES

## *Key Witness*

## *Book 6*

## *Bjorn Esterday Was Not Born Yesterday*

## Wynter Sommers

GJ dePillis

Published by Pure Force Enterprises, Inc.
California, USA
Since 2002

ISBN-13: 978-1-7184-0007-8
ISBN-10: 1-7184-0007-1

# DEDICATION

To all of us whose hearts reach out to change the world around, whose minds calculate the next strategic move, whose souls crave adventure and value the freedoms of democracy. To the spirit harnessing the power of fiction to alter our reality, making the world a better place for everyone.

# Bjorn Series Alternate Reading Plan

1st   Edges Book 1
2nd  Edges Book 2
3rd   Gone Book 1
4th   Firebrand Book 1
5th   Edges Book 3
6th   Firebrand Book 2
7th   Gone Book 2
8th   Gone Book 3
9th   Firebrand Book 3
10th  Gone Book 4
11th  Firebrand Book 4
12th  Gone Book 5
13th  Gone Book 6
14th  Edges Book 4
15th  Firebrand Book 5
16th  Gone Book 7
17th  Firebrand Book 6
18th  Gone Book 8
19th  Firebrand Book 7
20th  Gone Book 9
21st  Firebrand Book 8
22nd Gone Book 10
23rd  Gone Book 11
24th  Gone Book 12
25th  Gone Book 13
26th  Firebrand Book 9 (End)
27th  Gone Book 14
28th  Gone Book 15
29th  Gone Book 16
30th  Gone Book 17
31st  Gone Book 18 (End)
32nd Edges Book 5
33rd  Edges Book 6
34th  Edges Book 7
35th  Edges Book 8
36th  Edges Book 9 (End)

Wynter Sommers

# CONTENTS

# ACKNOWLEDGMENTS

To all those gentle souls who have graciously given tokens of love, hope, and kind considerations to others.

# 0 Preface

Skipper reveals his castle has a dungeon. Skipper Courtly also throws a tantrum on the construction scaffolding in his castle. He is fiercely possessive about his Stradivarius violin. Skipper demands to be locked in the dungeon so he can commune with the spirits to further his goal of harnessing supernatural powers. Skipper seems to want to gain superiority over other city rulers. Is it his ambition to take complete control of all the corporate cities?

Bjorn wants to bring dinner to Sarah's condo but when he arrives, he sees she has left him a note... she seems to still be back at work.

During Sarah's time at the job, she is injured.  Sarah ends up in the hospital.

# 1 CHAPTER Year 2036: Sammy Scribe's Office (Continuous Ch 53)

Bjorn Esterday, holding a cup of hot morning tea, walked toward his boss, who sat behind an imposing cluttered desk. Sammy Scribe, editor of The Daily Memo, interrupted Bjorn's discussion of the castle Lifestyles remodeling series.

Annoyed by the buzz of morning activity, Sammy got up to close his office door in order to block out the noise created by news staff rushing around to meet deadlines.

Sammy was trying to understand what Bjorn had just told him as he headed back to his seat.

"But, if Sarah had been dismissed from her job, she wasn't working for them anymore. So, who would tell her she had to report to the castle before she could get her final paycheck?"

Bjorn shrugged, "I know I was supposed to be doing a straight-forward celebrity story, but I just think there is more going on..."

Sammy retorted, "I find you a spot in Lifestyles. A rich celeb remodels his castle. Nice and cushy. Easy, really, and you uncover... this... stuff! I don't know if we should go to press with any of it."

"Look. I can pump out a piece on throne rooms, frescos and paint colors, Sammy. But, what I want to know is how Sarah ended up unconscious in the basement. What hit her so hard she got a concussion?"

"You said she was crawling on a high ledge," Sammy tried to use reason with Bjorn. "Maybe she accidentally sat up and banged her head on the ceiling. I mean why would anybody deliberately conk Sarah out? What would be the motive?"

Bjorn's thoughts raced.

"The foreman doesn't have a motive to hurt her. He'd just met her that morning. If Skipper knew anybody was in that dungeon with him, he'd kick her out accusing her of trying to steal the powers of his ghost. Pip wasn't around. I don't know who would want to do that to Sarah."

Frustrated, Bjorn slammed his beverage down on Sammy's desk, spilling a bit of the contents.

Sammy, understanding, pushed aside the cluttered papers, grabbed a sweater he had draped over the back of his chair, and started to mop up the spilt tea.

"Think, Bjorn. I know you miss investigative reporting, but you don't have a mystery here. And you are still not done with the Lifestyle-of-the-rich series. Besides, if this really was deliberate, who would put Sarah into a situation where she could have died? And why?"

## 2 CHAPTER Year 2036: Music supply shop a few days later. (Continuous Ch 54)

In the crowded music supply shop, Skipper Courtly instinctively pulled in his arms as he accidentally brushed against the common people also milling about looking at instruments and sheet music. He guarded the violin, still with its snapped string, protectively from the masses, sometimes walking close behind attorney Atsushi, in order to hide a bit.

Earlier, the lawyer had timidly suggested that Skipper might find it easier to carry the violin in its hard velvet-lined case, but Skipper brushed him aside angrily and barked, "Case, case, case. Never mind the case. Just get me to that music store, now! No time to waste. She needs repairs." Skipper cooed, cradling the wooden instrument.

When Atsushi suggested inviting a music store sales man to bring samples to Mr. Courtly's home, Skipper had screamed, "Junk, junk, junk. They only bring junk. That's why my string broke in the first place. I am not going through that, again! I want to inspect their entire stock."

Atsushi quietly capitulated and now here they were at the music store, as ordered.

Before looking through the merchandise cases, Atsushi had a sanitizer ready to apply to Skipper's hands as soon as he stuck his palms out.

With furrowed brow, Skipper Courtly blinked upwards with an expression of distress as he tried to control his own rapid breathing, which signaled to Atsushi to immediately provide another dose of sanitizer.

Atsushi had become most understanding and indulgent of the quirks of the Courtlys, father and son.

Gingerly, both Skipper and Atsushi approached the busy counter. Atsushi was careful to use his body to shield Skipper from accidental brushes with the commoners swarming casually about the store. Atsushi knew how his boss worked. This shop appeared to be short-staffed. Two harried employees raced about trying to fulfill their customers' demands by answering questions, grabbing items from stock, and ringing them up.

Skipper chided Atsushi, "I thought you said this place would be cleared out for me. How can I shop with these people?" Skipper rolled his eyes at the burden he had to endure.

Then a clerk, with "Joe" written on his name-tag, approached Skipper from behind the counter and smiled.

Skipper pre-empted Joe's greeting with,

"Clerk, I need to have my violin fixed."

Joe replied, "Sir, what exactly requires fixing?" Then Joe tried to look at the neck of the violin Skipper thrust in front of him. But Skip pulled the violin protectively away, preventing the clerk from even touching it.

"Do you need rosin? Neck repair?" Joe tried to guess since Skipper made it clear he was done talking and simply wiggled the violin mid-air with his eyes closed.

"Do you need an A-String? E-String?"

Skipper simply kept his eyes closed and rocked the violin in the air, one hand grasping the neck and one the body, refusing to let it go.

So, Joe left to assist a different customer who was waving for help.

Then, another clerk, "John", came by to wait on Skipper. He was about to offer assistance, but Skipper cut him off. Skipper barked at him, thinking John was Joe.

"Can't you see I need a G-sting?"

Skipper blustered.

Politely, John replied, "For your violin, Sir? Or are you looking for the lingerie shop next door?"

Skipper squinted at this man's face and demanded, "Where is the other one, Clerk Jim?"

"Jim? There isn't a Jim that works, here. Do you mean Joe?" Clerk John suggested helpfully.

Skipper, frustrated and embarrassed, looked around for the first man, spotting him with another client.

Skipper, turning red faced, shoved his violin into Atsushi's hands barking, "Here. You handle this."

And he stomped toward the exit.

Atsushi, now holding the violin, smiled apologetically at Clerk John as he watched Skipper storm out.

## 3 CHAPTER  Year 2036: Corp Party (Continuous Ch 55)

Bjorn Esterday, realizing the time, walked quickly into the Courtly Dynamics Corporation Lobby to get his visitor badge from the concierge desk. Cold marble slabs lined the floors and walls of this vast space. It was afternoon, by now, and he suspected some employees must still be on their lunch break because there were so few people around.

They made him stand to have his photo taken for a temporary holographic identification tag, which they efficiently affixed to his sports coat lapel. Per procedure, the receptionist rapidly programmed a small map-drone, which was then placed on the ground near Bjorn's feet.

The device was especially designed to escort visitors to their specified destinations on campus. It was small, close to the floor, with a large fat set of wheels underneath a box. It looked a little like a rounded toaster oven.

On top, was a weather proofed screen showing a map of the Courtly Corporation campus with the standard "You Are Here" symbol. The symbol on the map moved as the drone guided Bjorn to his appointment. The map drone travelled along the Courtly walkways and corridors, humming softly until the "You Are Here" indicator matched up with the "Your Destination" symbol.

Bjorn had been escorted to the Executive offices. Once the "Your Destination" and "You are Here" symbols coincided, a robotic voice stated, "You have arrived for your appointment with Mr. Skipper Courtly. Have a nice day."

The map-drone turned 180 degrees and returned, presumably, to its home base at the front desk of the imposing lobby.

Bjorn was taken aback to find that all the employees were in formal dress. The men were in black tie. The women wore long elegantly decorated gowns. Walking around were tall stunning models showing off the latest couture examples of the town's local fashion designers.

Realizing he was clearly under-dressed, Bjorn simply looked at his note taking device, perplexed. Across the room, Bjorn found Skipper Courtly, wearing the latest in tuxedo fashion, and surrounded by his fawning executives. Skipper was showing off the hand-crafted details of his tuxedo. Obviously, it was a new acquisition.

Pip looked sullen as he emerged from his executive office holding a violin case.

Bjorn made his way through the elegant crowd, dodging waiters who were carrying silver trays of drinks and appetizers. Bjorn approached Skipper and remarked, "Mr. Courtly, when I booked the appointment with your office, I wasn't told to show up in black tie."

Skipper ushered Bjorn away from the group and whispered. "Oh, oh, oh. My good man, I can't meet with you today. You see, I forgot we had an appointment. I didn't tell any of my guests what happened that day back at the castle. Best to keep it mysterious, don't you think?"

"Sir?" Bjorn replied.

"Off the record, Mr. Esterday. I am telling everyone that I have, in fact, already encountered and conquered the spirits of the dungeon. Shhhh," Skipper whispered as he silently requested Bjorn's compliance with his request for secrecy. Then, changing his tone of voice, he continued, "Of course, I had to wait to have my violin repaired before I could make a public announcement of my powers. I can't believe those clumsy workmen. Good help is hard to get, eh?"

"I'm not following, Mr. Courtly."

"We do not wish your visit to be wasted, but you cannot attend this party. We'll tell you what. While our soirée is in progress, you will be taken on a tour."

Skipper summoned a drone to go fetch an intern. The map drone obediently hummed off. Skipper headed back toward his adoring employees.

As Skipper turned away, an executive messenger intercepted him, whispering in his ear.

Mr. Courtly, annoyed said, "Leave my party, now? No, no, no..."

The messenger pleaded.

Acquiescing, Mr. Courtly said, "Fine. Fine. Fine. But hurry. Where are they set up?"

"Mr. Esterday," Skipper Courtly said as he and the messenger walked passed Bjorn, "Some friendly advice. Consult a tailor. The break of your crease is quite unfortunate."

Skipper's eyes swept disapprovingly over Bjorn's slacks. Then the messenger and Skipper Courtly walked off.

## 4 CHAPTER Year 2036: The Board Meeting (Continuous Ch 56)

Skipper Courtly was mildly surprised to see his entire Board of Directors assembled around a table.

"We need to know what to do about the employees who are on strike," one executive stated as Skipper sat down.

Another added, "They refuse to go back to work on the assembly lines. This is the fourth day. We've been able to keep it out of the news, so far, because the strike has been peaceful."

Skipper said, "Idiots, idiots, idiots. Cancel the worker's credits. That'll get them back to work."

"All their credits? But, if we cancel their credits, they won't be able to buy food. Is that ethically..."

Skipper, cutting him off retorted, "Morals. Morals. Morals. This is not a church, it's a business. Cut the credits!" Skipper demanded, "What else!"

The executives around the room glanced at each other.

"Next on our agenda is the law that we hope will be put into place. The World Unified Corporations will review it soon."

"What? What? What?" Skipper asked.

"The law to change the definition of 'employee' to 'asset', allowing us to depreciate them over five years to pay less and less as their value diminishes with use."

"That's accounting. No concern to me," Skipper snapped.

"Except for the final clause," the executive explained. "We need your signature on this to allow us to liquidate fully depreciated asset-employees to help improve our bottom line."

"Execute my workers? As in kill them? Who would do the work?" Skipper asked.

"Well, obviously we still need workers, but we'd only liquidate those that became a problem, like ones who instigate strikes. It is similar to the law that redefined a corporation as an individual. It would simply redefine an individual employee as an asset. This law will make it easier for us to remove those problem employees without all the cumbersome paperwork and investigations." The executive went on, "It makes it a Board of Directors decision and it makes it legal."

"And how do you plan to dispose of the bodies?" Skipper asked.

"Sir. That is a management detail we can work out once the World Unified Corporations makes it a law. Sign here to agree to the decision to change the definition of an 'employee' to an 'asset'."

Impatient, Skipper picked up the stylus, "Gentlemen, gentlemen, gentlemen. I hope this is all you needed me for. I must get back to my party!" And scribbled his signature on the electronic surface.

# 5 CHAPTER- Year 2036: Bjorn On Tour (Continuous Ch 57)

Bjorn, now huddled off in a corner with nothing but his note taking device to keep him company, was stuck waiting for some intern to give him a tour.

"I don't believe this," he said to himself. "You save a guy's life and not only do I NOT get a 'thank you', but I don't even get a follow up interview for which I made an appointment!"

A young woman, about age 18, entered the room, approached certain guests, and indicated an area near the exit where they should wait. One by one, they started to form a little group. Then, the young woman came to Bjorn.

"Hello. My name is Alexandra. I'm an intern here. Would you like to join our tour of the campus?"

Bjorn shrugged, "Sure."

Alexandra pointed toward the group by the door and said, "Lovely. In that case, please join those guests over there and I will be with you in a moment."

She curtsied and left before Bjorn could answer. Slowly, he forced himself to join the small, obviously well-heeled group, wishing he could just get this interview done.

To reach the exit, Bjorn had to pass by a circle of executives huddled together, drunk and giggling at private jokes. He recognized one of them, the attorney, Mr. Atsushi, as the one he had met on the stairs at Skipper's Castle.

An Earth Farmer boy approached the obviously drunk Atsushi. They spoke briefly. Atsushi patted the Earth Farmer boy on the head and dismissed him.

Bjorn watched the young man halt at

the exit, then turn and look back at the people in the room. Bjorn couldn't read his expression. Who was he looking at? Then the boy was gone.

Bjorn remembered that Sarah mentioned one of the interns was an Earth Farmer kid named Joshua Lantz. He wondered if this was the same boy. Had to be. Why would any Earth Farmer want to even consider interning at a corporation.

Bjorn watched Atsushi staggering to a small trashcan. The attorney took one handkerchief out of his pocket with a bandaged hand, dropping another used handkerchief onto the floor. As Atsushi wiped away tears of drunken laughter from his face, he scooped up both handkerchiefs and tossed them into the waste basket. One seemed to glint as if something shiny was inside.

Atsushi got distracted as his buddies called him over. Two of them flanked him, sweeping him back into their boisterous group, wanting to show Atsushi a printed newspaper article.

Bjorn recognized that it was yesterday's paper, but he was too far away to read the words. He just saw an image of a hot air balloon. He decided to look it up later. He was absorbed in his thoughts as he waited for the tour to start. He looked around at the tipsy formally dressed guests.

From this vantage point, Bjorn could see Pip, Skipper's son, leaning against the far wall, still holding the violin case. Then Pip casually walked to the temporary stage and placed the violin case near the microphone stand. Apparently, there'd be a performance later. Bjorn's thoughts were interrupted by the approach of the intern.

"My name is Alexandra and I will be your tour guide. Please follow me," and she led them out of the room.

# 6 CHAPTER  Year 2036: Violin Solo (Continuous Ch 58)

Bjorn had assumed Skipper would instruct an intern to give him a private tour. He was hoping he could milk the kid for information or even rumors. He was annoyed to find Skipper had done the easy thing and just added Bjorn's name to the list of an already scheduled group.

Alexandra had opened several doors along one corridor, to allow for easy viewing. The stiletto heels of the formally dressed women echoed against highly polished floors. Bjorn's rubber soled shoes squeaked a little with each step he took.

The troupe walked away from the cocktail party sounds. Suddenly all went quiet. Then just as quickly, the guests at the party burst into applause and cheers.

"Should we go back and join the fun?" Bjorn quipped to one of the tuxedo clad men. The man just shrugged and then hiccuped.

They were led into a small work room. The intern-tour-guide stopped and turned toward the group.

"This is the hobby room of one of the Courtly Dynamics Corporation executives. Through that door you will find his private office. If you go through that office, you will exit to where the party is right now."

"Hobby room with a burner?" one of the guests asked.

"It's all equipment for blowing glass," Alexandra explained. "I'm not an artist so I cannot demonstrate how it's done, but since Pip Courtly makes this room available to anybody who shares his artistic inclinations, I suppose I could learn, if I wanted to."

The small group chuckled.

In the distance, the cocktail party cheered again. Alexandra paused as the cheers died down.

"It is up to you. I am happy to continue with the tour, but I see several of you wondering what is happening back at the party, so would you like to continue the tour or would you prefer to return to the party and resume the tour later?"

Alexandra waited.

The guests murmured that they were curious as to what was happening back at the party, so Alexandra obliged and led them back.

A hush fell over the crowd inside the party room. Then, the scratchy playing of a woefully unpracticed violinist began. Screech, scrunch, squeak is how the violin sounded to everyone but Skip.

"Who is playing that?" another of the guests asked the tour guide.

"Uh. We are presented with a unique treat by our CEO, Skipper Courtly," Alexandra diplomatically shared.

Bjorn involuntarily flinched at the attempted musical notes piercing through the closed door. The party crowd inside responded as if Paganini were playing an instrument crafted by Antonio Stradivari himself.

Bjorn mused that the Stradivarius violin became synonymous with unequaled sound and quality, yet Skipper Courtly was unequaled in a very different sense of the word.

Muffled through the door, as the tour party approached, came a male voice thanking the audience.

"I can play even more notes!" Skipper, the encouraged violinist, announced.

Alexandra gently opened the door, leading her tour group back to re-join the soirée.

At that moment, the 'music' resumed and violin notes went up the scale until they reached an ear-shattering pitch. The violinist leaned his instrument into the microphone to amplify the effect. Skipper laughed delighted as he saw members of his audience covering their ears. He was strong. He was powerful. He could stun and amaze them all.

Then, abrupt silence.

Bjorn couldn't see the area Skipper Courtly performed at, but he did hear horrified gasps.

"What's wrong with him?"

"Why is he shaking?"

Attendees rushed to Skipper, who now, had dropped his beloved violin onto the stage floor. The CEO staggered, gasping for breath, shuddering. His eyes bulged as he tumbled into the audience and collapsed.

Bjorn noticed Pip across the room. Silent. Frozen. Alexandra, eyes wide, stared paralyzed.

Somebody sounded an alarm and immediately, medical personnel rushed in with equipment, shouting for guests to step back so they could tend to Skipper Courtly, who now lay motionless on the floor.

Some guests stayed to watch. Others fled the room, saying they needed to give the medics space to work.

Bjorn wandered to where Skipper had been performing. Something on the ground glittered in the light, catching his attention. The remaining guests focused on the progress of tending to Skipper.

Bjorn grabbed a clean napkin, opened it, and carefully took the end of his stylus to place tiny shards of clear glass up from the floor, into the center of the napkin, folding it closed, and placing it in his pocket.

He then ambled over to look inside an almost empty trashcan nearby. The blood spotted napkin was still there. Bjorn picked it up and placed it in his other pocket.

Bjorn glanced back. All eyes were on the medics, who were still desperately working on Skipper, trying to revive a lifeless body.

Was Skipper Courtly dead?

# 7 CHAPTER   Year 2036: A Person Of Interest (Continuous Ch 59)

Inside the comfort of her apartment, Sarah and Bjorn watched the news updates.

The death of Skipper Courtly was announced, and Pip was taken into custody as a "person of interest".

Sarah mused, "I wonder what that really means, to be a person of interest?" She looked at Bjorn, "I mean was it natural causes or do they suspect Skipper died from something else?"

Bjorn replied, "You are finally

discharged from that hospital and this is what you think about?"

"Well, no, silly," Sarah smiled, "I'm glad I'm home with my own things, on my own sofa, with my very own Bjorn Esterday, watching the news."

"There is something just not right about that story," Bjorn observed.

"What do you mean? You said it all happened so fast," Sarah commented.

Bjorn motioned to turn up the volume of the broadcast.

The news anchor was reporting, "...however, we have just learned that they are investigating the cause of death, and questioning Pip Courtly, his son, at Soldier Police headquarters."

The news co-host chimed in, "Will Pip inherit the Courtly Empire even if he is found guilty of murdering his own father?"

The first newscaster replied, "No criminal charges have been made and there have been no arrests."

"So several people have been questioned to assist the SP's with these inquiries?" the news co-host tossed back.

"Pip Courtly has just been asked to provide his insight and direction to the SP investigators," The first newscaster continued. "Nobody has even mentioned the word ARREST with COURTLY in the same sentence. Besides, Skipper Courtly could have passed away due to natural causes. They are still investigating."

Then cheerfully he looked directly into the camera and smiled at his TV audience adding, "Next in the news is the amazing story of a dog who summoned the Solider-Police to the aid of a little baby..."

Bjorn silenced the news with a wave of his hand. He got up and opened a communication channel on his com device.

Speaking briefly, he said, "Yeah. Can you do me a favor? Can you look at something for me?" he paused. "Sure. Now is fine. Great! I will be right there."

As Bjorn headed to the door, Sarah asked, "Where are you going?"

## 8 CHAPTER Year 2032: One Month After Earthshake at the Widow's Cloister (Continuous Ch 60)

From behind the cover of boulders and trees, four sisters crouched in a cart as the two Earth Farmers, on horseback, gazed down the hill at the distant Cloister beyond.

"When will it be safe," the Eldress whispered to Elder James, "to re-occupy our cloister?"

Elder James just shook his head sadly. He had a magnification device, and handed it to Eldress. She peered through the telescope at the Widow's Cloister,

35

which used to be her home.

It was now overrun by Anti-Corporatists. Some AnCors relaxing. Some eating from Queenie's courtyard garden. Some guarding. All occupying.

"They certainly took that literally," the Eldress whispered to Queenie.

"Took what literally?" Queenie inquired.

"That possession is nine tenths of the law," Eldress smiled.

"I've never heard that before. What does it mean?" Queenie whispered.

"It means, Child," the Eldress handed the magnification device back to Elder James as she gazed down at her now former home, "that those men with their weapons, have completely moved into our building, making it their own."

"What will you do, Eldress?" Elder James asked as he beckoned the ladies to step away from the ridge in case they were seen.

"Let it be."

"What?" Queenie asked startled, "You mean you don't want to instruct such fellows to leave? You're letting them..."

Eldress spoke softly, "Child. Those AnCors won't simply say 'Oh, pardon me, our mistake, we'll move out.' It's just not in their nature. No. We are not warrior women. We must have faith that God will provide. It's not giving up. It's trusting in a God who sees the entire picture."

"But it's not..." Queenie protested.

"When God answers prayers," Eldress interrupted, "He resolves several issues, not just our need to live somewhere. We must pray and give God time to work out our future."

Eldress climbed back up into the wagon. "You are not the only one who has lost your home. We must be thankful all the sisters and widows got out alive, thanks to the warnings of Elder James. Be thankful and appreciative when you can. It makes every situation so much easier for everyone to bear."

Feeling admonished, Queenie dragged her feet as she also climbed into the cart. The horse readied itself to clomp slowly back to Elder James' monastery.

Queenie sat, hands folded in her lap, feeling very small and very tired as the cart and the other horses moved along.

Eldress leaned toward Queenie. "Anybody you ask today would say they didn't envision their current life for themselves. They'd want more health, less sickness; more peace, less war, more money, less poverty; more loving family, less loneliness." Putting a hand on Queenie's shoulder, Eldress said softly, "We all must plow through the situations given to us and see if there is something we can appreciate once we work through those circumstances."

Eldress hoped it would comfort Queenie.

Queenie sighed, resigned. It was time to find a new home. Silently, she held her single quilt square, knowing she must have left the other piece back inside the cloister, probably carelessly tossed away by now. She will never see that scrap of fabric, nor her garden, again.

She couldn't explain how she felt to these Earth Farmer brothers and sisters. They would simply say she was attaching too much meaning to a material object. It's best she forget about that other quilt square, anyway. Best to forget the past and just focus on the future.

## 9 CHAPTER Year 2032: The Rest Haven Village (Continuous Ch 61)

"Aren't we heading back to the monastery?" Eldress asked Elder James, who was leading the small party. She noticed they were not backtracking on the same path.

"I wish to show you something, first."

"Will we return in time for supper?" Eldress asked him, then turned to Queenie, "I do not know where he leads us, but I do trust him to get us back in time. Isn't that right, Elder James?"

"Yes," Elder James said simply.

After another hour of riding, Elder James led the Earth Farmer party into a small deserted village. Clearly, this place had been abandoned for some time.

One of the brothers helped Eldress out of the cart. Elder James beckoned for Eldress to follow him. He walked to a well in the center of what used to be a town. There was an old bucket there, and they lowered it into the pit. Up came a full bucket of water.

Another brother turned to Queenie and helped her out of the cart, as well. Soon they were all gathered at the well.

"The water is cool," Eldress stated, then sipped from the bucket edge, "and sweet to drink. Here, try some."

She passed the bucket around. Each person took a sip of cool sweet pure water. It was a refreshing break.

One brother took the bucket and drank sloppily, "So sorry, I didn't realize how thirsty I was, Elder," he said, red faced, as he passed the bucket along.

"It is a restful haven after our long journey, Eldress," Elder James stated, smiling.

"Rest Haven. Indeed," Eldress replied with a gentle smile.

Elder James and Eldress wandered away from the well, exploring the abandoned buildings as they chatted quietly, away from the rest of the group.

Queenie, watching them from across the center of this ghost town, leaned over to one of the brothers, "What do you think they are talking about, brother?" she asked.

"I can only surmise, Widow Medicina," he said.

"What is your guess?" Queenie urged.

"I think," the brother started as he looked at them from a distance, "that they are assessing if this will be your new home or not."

"What?" Queenie asked.

# 10 CHAPTER Year 2033: Rest Haven Village Months Later (Continuous Ch 62)

All the sisters who used to inhabit the cloister and the Earth Farmer brothers, including Elder James, wore rough work clothes. There was still much to do in this isolated, formerly abandoned village, to make it habitable.

Queenie painted a sign which read, "Earth Farmer Rest Haven Inn for Weary Travelers".

"Nicely done, Child," Eldress said as Queenie finished up with the final strokes of paint.

"We travelled here weary. You called it a rest haven when we first saw this place. I figured if we can provide rest for others... then..." Queenie explained.

"You've learned a great lesson. I'm very pleased," Eldress smiled kindly and left to check on the progress of the others.

One of the sisters came by to take a break after some heavy work. "Look at what I found," she announced. "It's an old mirror," she smiled at Queenie. "Widow Medicina, would you like it?"

"Oh, no. I don't need to be looking at myself. Give it to Elder James for the Inn's guests," Queenie replied.

"So," the sister continued, dropping the mirror into her apron pocket, "do you think the neighboring villages will know where we are?"

Queenie replied, "I'm sure word will travel fast. We are near some clear landmarks if they simply look around. It won't take them long to find the place."

"I'll bet you're wanting to get another garden planted, soon, eh?" the sister smiled.

"As soon as we get the basics done. I'll see if we can trade for some small trees I can transplant here. If we cannot grow fruit or vegetables this season, then..."

"Then," a brother came by also to rest, overhearing the conversation, "then, God will give the monastery plenty in our crops to share with you. Or we can trade with other villages for food this season."

"Perhaps," the sister chimed in, "but, I think we will need to get very creative to earn an income to maintain this place."

"I've just painted a sign," Queenie commented. "Eldress suggested that we could take in travelers who need rest and a meal."

"The brothers can help you run that, as well," the brother offered. "Who knows, maybe it would grow to be profitable. Next time I trade with the villages nearby, I will share with the others that there is a new lodge for any weary visitors that those villages cannot accommodate. An alternative."

"There is much to do, then," Queenie stated as she got up and headed toward the center courtyard.

"Widow Medicina, what...?" the sister asked Queenie.

Over her shoulder Queenie replied, "We have a chapel to set up, gardens to plant, and maybe we will convert a building into a school for the children from other villages."

The brother looked at the sister. "I suppose if Widow Medicina is working, we should get back to work, as well. Elder James wants me to see if we can set up some sort of plumbing."

"But, won't all that take so much effort and time?" the sister asked as her limbs seemed heavy and resistant to doing any further work.

"It's your new home, Sister. It looks like Widow Medicina, there, is planning on inviting every weary soul to visit."

## 11 CHAPTER Year 2035: War Torn Village Slave Children (Continuous Ch 63)

The AnCor wars had continued to wreak havoc on the smaller villages, which did not have the resources to recover as quickly as the bigger corporation-owned-cities. Yet, the benefit of being in such a village was that Jack Courtly now had the luxury of remaining incognito.

Since escaping from prison, Jack had spent the last three years learning to survive on his own. His skin had become leathery, his beard coarse, his eyes

49

darted about anticipating the next attack, his frame became powerful from the labors he undertook to survive. He would never now be recognized as that once elegantly dressed businessman.

Depressed at the loss of his family, he wandered randomly, berating himself for not having protected his wife and child on that terrible day. Memories of them pained him. Whenever he thought of his only child, Ace, and beloved wife Queenie, tears stung his eyes, blurring his vision. By now, he had lost hope of ever seeing them again.

He was keenly aware of Skipper's malicious feelings about him. It would be easy for Skipper, now a man of unlimited resources, to snuff out the life of a man who now had none. He couldn't go home.

Jack's manners ingratiated him into the homes of small villages needing handy-man services. He learned to fight off desperate gangs of marauders. He learned to evade AnCors and SP's alike. He often slept in the open, in the crook of a forest tree, or in desolate abandoned buildings. At other times, he was able to find a stable with fresh hay to sleep on.

There was a class Jack had never given much thought to, the vagrant class. He used to think they were lazy and chose that life. Now, he realized that sometimes that life trapped you into a living situation you just had to get used to, to survive.

This particular village was home to many neglected people, who didn't bathe regularly, and perhaps only owned one or two sets of clothes per person. This was not the luxurious lifestyle that Jack Courtly had grown up with, yet it was here that he hoped to find safety for one more night.

He looked around as he stumbled across this new village.

He had been on the move for quite a while now. He had gone back to observe the Cloister several times, only to find that it was still occupied by AnCors.

He didn't want to move far from the former Widow's Cloister, and at times convinced himself that the woman who looked like Queenie, might be nearby. He needed to talk to her. He fought off thoughts of having invented the encounter with her at the men's prison.

He took a deep breath. No. It couldn't have been Queenie. His family was dead and he had to embrace that fact and move on with his life. Right now, his priority was to stay alive. He should stop this mad senseless search for a family he knew was gone.

Exhausted, he stumbled along the dusty village street with no particular destination in mind, yet always alert for possible AnCor attacks.

Jack reasoned that perhaps the AnCors started from some group of legitimately disgruntled employees who worked for abusive corporations. He had heard stories of companies in the early 21st century stealing the pensions from retired workers; or cheating customers by feigning positive financial reports, yet emptying their accounts; or giving large amounts of pay to executives who not only avoided work, but greedily stole and murdered to cripple the very corporations they worked for.

Jack was convinced none of his Courtly corporations had been run that way while he had been at the helm. But, he understood why the AnCor movement got started... There was, he now had to admit, no other way for the common man to fight the abuse and corruption that permeated the ruling classes.

Even before the AnCor's inception, the government funded justice system was collapsing, becoming privatized, and leaving enforcement of justice to the whim of corporate executives. This shift of judicial enforcement allowed for the rise of the unorganized and increasingly vicious AnCors.

Suddenly, a local villager ran into the road screaming, "Slavers! Slavers! Hide the children!"

And just as quickly, this villager disappeared into one of the huts. Everyone else responded immediately by grabbing children who were playing in the street and physically dragging them indoors.

Jack ducked behind the cover of some old barrels in the alleyway between two buildings. He knew slave auctions occurred in large villages, and he never forgot that he himself nearly got sold into slavery when he was captured at the AnCor camp. Now that the AnCors had moved into the cloister, they must be raiding the local villagers of their children to raise money for their cause.

Jack knew the one important source of income for the AnCors' was selling of human slaves, as well as acts of terror-for-hire.

With practiced efficiency, an old fashioned formerly gasoline-powered truck, now retrofitted to use the fuel available in today's modern world, roared into the main street of the town, kicking up dust as it screeched to a halt. The back bed was altered into a large cage, already filled with children from other villages the AnCors had visited earlier that day.

This was how the AnCors harvested before they went to market. To them, slavery was just a business. In their minds, they justified it as a necessary step to financially support their ideals of freedom.

Out jumped two scruffy AnCors racing around, banging on doors, demanding children or threatening destruction. Another AnCor stayed in the truck, behind the wheel.

Jack remained hidden as he watched. He was a newcomer here and didn't want to get involved. He was tired and now only wanted to stay alive.

A spiteful AnCor started a fire at one of the structures, frustrated that the people inside refused to produce any children to be sold. An angry villager anticipated this move and immediately poured boiling liquid from the top floor, scalding the man who set the fire. Instantly, villagers raced out into the street already prepared with buckets of water to extinguish the blaze, then retreated to safety.

Jack liked that this village, although poor and shabby, really pulled together against the odds. Maybe he could make this his new home for a while.

The scalded AnCor, screaming, staggered back to the slave truck. The driver waiting there was unmoved by his fellow AnCor's plight, believing destiny had determined the stumbling man's fate, so it was not his place to interfere.

"Stop. You are wounded!" came a very familiar voice. "You can not return to camp with us, fool," was the order. The scalded AnCor was collared and dragged down onto the ground by none other than Percy Snatcher.

Jack stared in disbelief.

Why would so many men work with self-sacrificing devotion for such a heartless, calculating, mercenary leader? Jack surmised that perhaps these foot soldiers never knew a family, never understood right from wrong, and were vulnerable to psychological puppeteering.

Jack recalled that when he was in the

men's prison, he learned Percy Snatcher might have had an undiagnosed case of prosopagnosia, which prevented Percy from recognizing faces.

In prison, Jack had decided to keep a low profile and Percy eventually ignored Jack, clearly forgetting Jack's true identity.

Jack was relieved he had taken and destroyed the photo of himself back when he had been held captive at the AnCor camp. There was nothing to remind Percy of who Jack really was. After Jack grew his beard, Percy definitely no longer recognized him.

Jack watched Percy stomp off, pausing only to kick the injured man out of his way.

"We have an auction in two days and still have four more villages to hit," Percy snapped, uncaring if anybody heard him. It was just business.

"You stay here. We don't have enough medical supplies for a fool who would get himself injured by the villagers he is raiding!"

"But," the man in anguish gasped, "you cannot leave me at the mercy of this village you just ordered me to burn!"

"I said this is business, fool. I can and I will." Percy stormed away. The driver just sat there, expressionless, as if this was a regular occurrence.

"Help me, Snatcher. You owe me!" the scalded AnCor pleaded stumbling after Percy.

Percy snapped, "You didn't harvest any slaves!"

Percy ordered the driver, "Keep the engine running! Leave only on my orders!"

The wounded man collapsed to his knees, pleading, "Please. They'll kill me!"

Percy spun around and spat, "Perfect. They'll save me the trouble."

The villagers looked out from the safety of their barricaded homes. They saw one dusty street. One weeping scalded AnCor.

One bored driver. And one angry slave driving business man whose sense of "right" was tied to what would make a profit.

From behind his protective cover, Jack watched appalled as Percy collared two new children. One in each hand. He roughly threw them against the back of the truck.

There might not be anything Jack could do to help the children already locked up, but he could do something to stop any new children from getting yanked away from their families. There was a chance that Jack would be taken and sold in their place, but he had to try.

Percy struggled with the terrified youths as he unlocked the cage. The other children inside the cage were already shackled, silent and numb with fear.

Percy yanked the cage door open and prepared to shackle these two new children. Jack lifted an empty barrel overhead and sent it flying where it smashed into the side of the truck. Percy spun around toward the noise. Then, Jack rushed in from behind.

The driver watched him, curious.

Jack wrapped a powerful arm around Percy's neck. Percy retaliated by kicking backwards. Jack side-stepped, avoiding getting his knee caps smashed by Percy's heel. Now Percy had both fists up, facing the bearded stranger. Adrenaline pumped through Jack's veins.

Percy shifted his weight to strike. Jack dropped, then drove his clenched fist upward, slamming into Percy's chin. The AnCor shrieked with pain as his head snapped back. Percy lost his grip on the two children.

Jack shouted, "Run!" at the stunned children.

One child took off. The other struggled to get away, but was trapped by the shackle already around one wrist.

Percy lunged at Jack with wild punches. Jack staggered back.

Percy looked at the driver, pointing and

shouting orders to him, exposing the brachial plexus at the top corner of his underarm. Jack took advantage of this brief opportunity and reached in to punch Percy's shoulder with a slight upward fisted jab. Percy felt a shock of electricity as his outstretched arm collapsed.

Percy shouted to the driver, "Get over here! Help me!" The driver seemed not to hear.

Percy punched Jack twice with the arm that was not rendered useless by Jack's electric blow. Jack rushed in and smacked the side of Percy's ear with his left hand while coming up with the back of his right hand to slam him on his chin, jarring the tiny "mental nerve" between the corner of Percy's mouth and his chin. This sharp, precise strike made Percy reel.

Jack whipped around, kicking Percy in the stomach with his heel. Percy staggered backwards, clawing at the side of the truck for support, but missing it and falling down.

Percy dropped the keys as he tried to break his own fall. The keys landed just out of reach of the partially shackled child who strained to grasp them. Jack pinned Percy down, choking him with a fury and rage he didn't know he had, while kicking the keys toward the child.

The youth unlocked his shackle with shaking hands. Once free, the boy tossed the keys inside the cage then raced away.

Jack felt Percy go limp.

The caged children scrambled and fought each other to get at the keys.

Jack jumped up, reached inside the cage, grabbed the keys and began to unlock each shackle, one at a time. As each shackle fell away, Jack gruffly tossed the freed child off the truck.

Those children Jack liberated scurried toward the village buildings. Doors briskly opened, the children were pulled inside, and the doors protectively slammed behind them.

Percy rolled to his hands and knees, as

Jack, now inside the cage, was freeing the very last child. Percy slammed the cage door behind Jack, trapping him inside with the remaining child.

Percy shouted at the driver, "Move out. Move out!", as he raced to the cab and pulled open the passenger door. Percy said, "We still got one adult and one kid for market."

Gears grinding as the truck's engine revved, the driver stepped on the pedal and the truck pulled out. The truck picked up speed, kicking up a cloud of dust.

Then, the shackles fell off. Jack, still holding the keys, grabbed the child with his free hand, and unlocked the cage door.

Jack engulfed the small, terrified child in his arms and jumped.

## 12 CHAPTER Year 2035: After Jack Jumped (Continuous Ch 64)

As Jack hit the ground, he released his grip and rolled over onto his back, winded. The child lay for a moment, stunned, then got up and ran.

Percy had lost his entire cargo.

Painfully, Jack sat up.

His head rested in his hands.

Jack shuddered when he realized he could have brought trouble to this innocent village. Had his foolishly heroic act actually revealed Jack's identity to the driver and would that driver tell Percy? Would Percy retaliate by returning to this village for Jack, destroying the little community to prove a point?

If Percy figured this village was too much trouble and would cost him his cargo again, the AnCors might not return. But, if Percy thought it was Jack Courtly he had just encountered, he would come back just for Jack, fueled by revenge and with reinforcements.

Jack didn't know if Percy ever got paid for murdering him or not. It would be safer for the village for Jack to move on.

The villagers now started coming out of their homes.

The men surrounded the scalded AnCor, binding his wrists and ankles.

Then, they approached Jack.

The villager who had signaled the slavery warning came up to Jack. This villager brought the two local children, a boy and a girl, who had almost been captured by the slavers.

"My sister and I wanted to say thank you," the young boy said.

Jack now had time to look at these faces. They both appeared to be about ten or eleven years old. Jack once had a child about that age years ago. A child and a wife. Both dead. At least they were spared from a life of slavery. Oh, how he missed Ace and Queenie.

The parents of the brother and sister brought Jack into their home, tended to Jack's wounds, and then fed him. Other households offered beds and meals to the other children Jack had rescued. They would rest, now.

Plans were made to return them to their villages in the morning.

The villagers asked Jack where he was headed and would he consider making their village his permanent home? Jack, without explaining to them why, said he had to move on. Before he left, he wanted to make sure the villagers were aware of how the AnCors worked and shared what he knew about them. This should somewhat help the villagers defend against future attacks.

Concerned he might endanger the

village for every additional moment he stayed, he said he had to leave immediately.

One man gave Jack a map.

"On your journey," the villager explained, "you may want to stop here. We hear this place takes in weary travelers. But, we insist, you spend at least one night to recuperate from your ordeal."

Jack accepted the map, folding it into his pocket. The place was a day or two away by foot. Jack spent the night in a bed for the first time in months.

The next morning, the appreciative villagers packed Jack a small bag of food from their meager supplies.

"Sir, you are a man of few words and we don't mean to intrude, but what may we call you so that we can welcome you in our homes again?" one villager asked politely.

"My name is not important, but thank you for your congenial hospitality. All of you. Thank you."

And Jack turned away.

Jack headed out in the brightening dawn, hoping that by nightfall, he could reach the place on the map and stay another night in a bed.

After several hours of walking, Jack sat to rest and eat by the side of the road. Overcome by exhaustion, he thought he should have taken the villagers kind offer to stay with them for a few more days and rest. He couldn't keep his eyes open any longer and Jack fell asleep under a tree.

He awoke to being kicked by youths stealing his bag of food and running off. Jack got up, but didn't have it in him to chase them. They were probably starving, he reasoned as he turned away and stood up.

Pangs of hunger, that sick feeling your gut experiences when it seems like it'll turn inside out, had become a familiar sensation for Jack.

Alone, along the desolate road, Jack stumbled.

He heard a wheeled vehicle approach from behind him. The official lights shining brightly gave him comfort. At least it wasn't an AnCor. It was too new and hummed softly with the sounds of solar power. It wasn't noisy like those gasoline powered antiques the AnCors drove. It rolled to a stop, as tires crunched over dry leaves, making more noise than the engine.

Jack figured he should hide, just the same, not realizing how he staggered. He tripped as he tried to find cover in the shrubbery to the side of the road.

The last thing he remembered was hearing a vehicle door close and footsteps approach.

\*\*\*\*\*\*\*\*\*\*

## 16 CHAPTER- What will happen next?

Pip Courtly, Skipper's son, is brought into the Soldier Police Headquarters as a "person of interest" in the case involving the  death of his father.

It Is the year 2032. Elder James brings the Sisters and Widows to an isolated abandoned village after rescuing them from the Widows' Cloister. He suggests they settle in this new place.

After some hard work, they have created a "Rest Haven village" and try to set up an Inn to earn money by taking in weary travelers.

One year after that, in 2033, we see that it has taken months of toil and labor, but the Earth Farmers and sisters have worked together to make a very nice comfortable village.

What will happen to Pip?

Is he innocent or guilty in Skipper's death?

Will  Sarah move to uncover the truth- even if it exonerates Pip Courtly, the man who fired her?

Will Bjorn act like an investigative reporter, or will he respect the safety net of the Daily Memo Newspaper and stay below the radar? Will he comply with Sammy Scribe's order to focus on writing a fussy decorative celebrity lifestyles piece? Or, will he, instead,  keep digging into the sordid mysteries of the Courtly family? We see how Queenie has adapted, but what about Jack? Where is he?

## ❧ To Be Continued... ☙

## 17 Did You Know

Some closed communities in America are not allowed to operate electrical equipment. For example, if they own a cheese factory, they would have to hire people from other areas to operate the electrical cheese factory equipment for them.

In EDGES, the Earth Farmers are a fictitious group.  They blend elements of Shakers, Amish, and Mennonite cultures to create the God-respecting Earth Farmers. concept of being self sufficient by combining godly faith, with agricultural farming and engineering and science.  By collaborating in all skills, it is realistic to  create a livable town in a few months.

What elements are needed for a low-tech, middle-class group of people, like the Earth Farmers, to turn a ghost town into a thriving,  comfortable community?

An American immigrant named Dr. Marcin Jakubowski created a "blue print" for civilization. Using open source ecology plans and knowledge-sharing, he is collecting plans to build simple mechanisms to start up a little town from scratch, including the efficient use of farming equipment.

They ask engineers to collaborate and come up with a version of the item that can be built easily and cost-effectively. Then, they need to test it and once the bugs in the design are worked out, it can be replicated and made available to the public.

According to Jakubowski, the Civilization Starter Kit includes:
1.  Dairy milkers
2.  Bakery ovens
3.  Wind turbines

4.  Tractors
5.  Building structures (a tiny home may take about 7 days to build)
6.  Solar connectors
7.  Hydraulic motors, etc

Schedule for Tiny Home in 7 Days :
  ✓    Day 1: press bricks, nail door and window frames and lay down the brick floor.
  ✓    Day 2: raise frames and stack bricks for walls and start on basic utilities.
  ✓    Day 3: finish walls and plaster and build other modules.
  ✓    Day 4: build roof modules and install other modules, then plaster walls.
  ✓    Day 5; Install roof, install basic utilities, paint siding.
  ✓    Day 6: place windows in window frames. Install doors on hinges. Install siding and trims.
  ✓    Day 7: Finish up the interior and finish up the exterior. Test the utilities. Done.

Before an inventor can share an innovation with the public, they  must be ORGANIZED.

Let's examine one model of DIY (Do It Yourself) hardware called a "civilization toolkit" .

A Polish immigrant to the United States, Marcin Jakubowski, got a PhD and felt useless.  He bought a farm and a tractor, but the tractor broke down. He paid to fix it, but it broke again... and soon he found himself "broke".  He thought there must be a better way, and if he was suffering, others in the United States, must be suffering as well.  Now that he was a U.S. Citizen, he firmly believed he had an obligation to do something to benefit his American neighbors.

Mr. Jakubowski decided to build a better, cheaper tractor. He not only did that, but he put the blue prints, estimated costs to build, budget plans, available to the public in a clear, easy-to-follow instructional manner. Soon, he found several others who also wanted to contribute to the open source model of, what he terms a "civilization starter toolkit". He has built and tested less than a dozen machines so far, but has received plans for over 120 and that number is growing.

Mr. Jakubowski's invention was good, even helpful, but if he presented it in a sloppy manner, others would not want to look at it. It takes more than just a good idea to ignite passion to create. It takes presenting that good idea in a clear ORGANIZED manner where the public can get something of value for free. This will help them become independent.

## ABOUT Wynter Sommers

Wynter Sommers is the pseudonym for an American writing team, which harnesses multiple skills in technology, research, and education. Formally trained with a PhD in Education, Wynter Sommers blends academic classroom experience, with corporate sophistication, and a passion for developing more effective student insights.

Wynter Sommers has taught classrooms of enthusiastic children. She has a heart to inspire creativity and develop critical thinking skills, all to encourage students to make wise choices in life. She wants to impart the talent of honing one's skills in self-reliance and collaborative team work. Despite any environmental barriers outside of an individual's control, Wynter Sommers wishes to impart the message that genuine hope, love, and peace can help us overcome obstacles, and cement friendships. Wynter Sommers hopes you enjoy the other ***Bjorn Esterday Was not Born Yesterday*** stories in this series.

www.ingramcontent.com/pod-product-compliance
Lightning Source LLC
Chambersburg PA
CBHW051841020726
47502CB00005B/1902